Brookie and Her Lamb

BROOKIE AND HER LAMB

M. B. Goffstein

The New York Review Children's Collection
New York

This is a New York Review Book
Published by the New York Review of Books
435 Hudson Street, New York, NY 10014
www.nyrb.com

Library of Congress Cataloging-in-Publication Data
Names: Goffstein, M. B., author, illustrator.
Title: Brookie and her lamb / by M. B. Goffstein.
Description: New York : New York Review Books, [2021] | Series:
    New York Review children's collection | Summary: Originally
    published: New York : Farrar, Straus and Giroux, 1967.
Identifiers: LCCN 2020012193 | ISBN 9781681375458 (hardcover)
Subjects: CYAC: Sheep—Fiction. | Animals—Infancy—
    Fiction. | Human-animal relationships—Fiction.
Classification: LCC PZ7.G5573 Br 2021 | DDC [E]—dc23
LC record available at https://lccn.loc.gov/2020012193

ISBN: 978-1-68137-545-8

Printed in the United States of America on acid-free paper.
10 9 8 7 6 5 4 3 2 1

To Joceline

Brookie had a little lamb
and she loved him very much.

Brookie taught the lamb to sing

and he had a very good voice,

but all he could sing was
Baa baa baa

so she taught him how to read,

and all he could read was
Baa baa baa

but she loved him anyhow.

Brookie took the lamb for a walk

and a little dog barked at them.

The lamb ate some flowers in the park

and they came home again.

Then Brookie made the lamb a room

with straw and pillows on the floor.

She gave the lamb a music book

with songs that he could sing,

and all the songs said
Baa baa baa

so he sang them very well.

She made the lamb a cozy place

where he could sit and read,

and all his books said
Baa baa baa

so he liked them very much.

Brookie loved her little lamb

and she scratched him behind his ears.

The little lamb said
Baa baa baa

and snuggled close to her.

ABOUT THE AUTHOR-ARTIST

M. B. Goffstein was born in St. Paul, Minnesota in 1940. She graduated from Bennington College and moved to New York City where she began writing and illustrating books for children and adults beginning with *The Gats!* (1966) and ending with *A House, A Home* (1989). She died in 2017 having spent her last decades writing fiction, painting, and photographing objects that delighted her.